The New Friend

by Kim Kane
Illustrated by Jon Davis

PICTURE WINDOW BOOKS
a capstone imprint

*For my dear friend Jane C-R and
her lovely Skye. And for Martha,
my 3-foot muse, to whom Ginger
owes every ounce of her vim.*

– Kim

Picture Window Books are published by Capstone,
1710 Roe Crest Drive, North Mankato, Minnesota 56003
www.mycapstone.com

Text Copyright © 2016 Kim Kane
Illustration Copyright © 2016 Jon Davis
Series Design Copyright © 2016 Hardie Grant Egmont
First published in Australia by Hardie Grant Egmont 2016
Published in American English in 2018 by Picture Window Books,
a Capstone imprint.

Editorial Credits
Alesha Sullivan, editor; Mack Lopez and Russell Griesmer, designers;
Laura Manthe, production specialist

Library of Congress Cataloging-in-Publication Data
Library of Congress Cataloging-in-Publication data is available on the
Library of Congress website.
978-1-5158-1946-2 (library binding)
978-1-5158-1952-3 (paperback)
978-1-5158-2014-7 (eBook PDF)

Printed in Canada.
010393F17

Table of Contents

Chapter One

My name is Ginger Green.

I am seven years old.

I am the Playdate Queen!

This afternoon, my friend Skye is coming over.

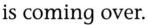

Skye is my new friend from
ballet. Skye has never been
to my house.

Skye does not know
that my house is tall
like a tree house.

Skye does not know that my bed
is tall like a stage.

Last Saturday at ballet, I said,
"Skye, I am Ginger Green,
Playdate Queen. Would you like
to come and play with me?"

Skye turned pink.

After class, Skye's dad said,

"YES!"

At twelve o'clock, the
doorbell rings.

DING
DONG!

It is Skye and her dad.

Mom says,

"Come in!"

Skye comes in.

Skye's dad comes in too.

"I'll just wait until the girls
are happy," says Skye's dad.

"Sure," says Mom.

She smiles, but I can see that
Mom is not happy.

Saturday is for making beds.

Saturday is for reading the paper.

Mom does not want to make coffee for Skye's dad.

"What do you want to play?"
I ask Skye.

I don't know what my new friend
Skye likes to do.

Skye turns pink.

Skye says nothing.
She looks at her
boots.

"Skye likes
to play
dress-up,"
says Skye's
dad.

"Great," I say. "I am Ginger Green, Playdate Queen!

I LOVE dress-up."

I open the dress-up box.

Skye takes a pointy hat and
a wand.

"I am a

witch," she says.

Skye's dad laughs.

I put on a pirate hat and a swishy skirt. I grab a parrot and a sword.

"I am Ginger Green, Pirate Queen," I yell.

"Arrrrr, me hearties,"

says Skye's dad.

I stop.

I feel my cheeks turn **pink**.

"Don't mind me," says Skye's dad.

Skye's dad is kind, but it's
to play dress-up with a dad in
the room.

I don't feel like a Pirate Queen.
I **cannot**
find the voice.

Chapter Two

Mom hands Skye's dad a cup of coffee. He says thanks.

"Let's go to my room," I say.

We go to my bedroom.

It is actually **our** bedroom.

I share it with my big sister Violet.

Violet is reading on the bed. Violet likes to read.

"Hi," says Skye's dad.

"Hi," says Violet.

She has to.

Violet can ignore me. And Violet does ignore me.

But Violet cannot ignore a grown-up.

Violet looks at me.

Her eyebrows are

HUNCHED.

I can tell Violet thinks it is weird that Skye's dad is here.

I think it's weird Skye's dad is here.

"Shall I go?" asks Skye's dad.

"Stay," says Skye.

Skye does not think it is weird.

I sit on the floor near my dollhouse.

Skye sits on the floor.

Skye's dad sits on the floor too.

His knees come up past his chin.

I try to **ignore** Skye's dad.

I try to **ignore** his knees.

I pick up the dolls.

"Do you want to be the mom or the dad?"

I ask Skye.

"The mom," says Skye.

"The mom please," says Skye's dad.

I pick up the baby.

I pick up the big sister.

But I am **NOT** in the mood.

It is hard to play with Violet
in the room.

It is harder to play with Skye's dad in the room.

I cannot find the voices.

I put the dolls down.

Skye is my new friend.

New friends are tricky.

I do not know
what new
friends like.

I look around.

I see Skye's ballet tights.

I see my tights.

I do know Skye LOVES dancing.

I LOVE dancing.

We both LOVE dancing.

We must dance!

Chapter
Three

I get up. "Let's dance," I say.

"We can have a dance party!"

Skye smiles.

Violet gets up.

"It is too **hard** to read in here," she says.

"I am going to the kitchen."

Skye looks at her dad.

Skye's dad looks at Skye.

I turn on some music.

I turn it up LOUD.

It is fun music.

It makes me want to JUMP.

It makes me want to KICK.

It makes me want to
WAVE my arms.

I am Ginger Green,

DISCO
QUEEN!

I love to dance.

Skye stands up.

Skye JUMPS to the music.

Skye KICKS to the music.

Skye WAVES her
arms to the music.

Skye's dad stands up.

He JUMPS to the music.

He does BIG jumps
with his
BIG
knees.

I am Ginger Green, Disco Queen, but it is too **hard** to dance with Skye's dad in the room.

I stop. Skye stops too.

Skye *rolls* her eyes.

"You can go now, Dad," says Skye.

"Are you sure?" asks Skye's dad.

Skye gives him a little push.

"It is **hard** to dance with a dad in the room," she says.

Skye's dad gives her a kiss.

"I am a **good** dancer," he says.

"Very good," says Skye. "But
Ginger Green is the Disco Queen."

"Skye is a disco queen too!"

I shout.

I JUMP

up on my bed.

It is tall like a stage.

My new friend Skye takes off her boots and JUMPS up on the bed too.

She smiles.

Her smile is big and happy.

Her smile is as happy as the music.

"I'll be back at three o'clock,"
says Skye's dad.

"See you at three!"

Skye shouts.

"See you at three!" I shout.

Then we **turn up** the music even louder.

We **KICK** even higher.

We **JUMP** even higher too.

My new friend Skye is sometimes
a bit shy.

My new friend Skye is sometimes
a bit scared.

But my new friend
Skye LOVES to dance.

I am Ginger Green, Playdate Queen, and I LOVE play dates.

Play dates with new friends are
a bit like a PUZZLE.

Sometimes
it just takes
time to work
out what
friends like.

My new friend Skye needs her
dad to start.

But my new friend Skye

LOVES

to dance.

My new friend Skye loves to dance with me.

THE END

Glossary

ballet—a performance that uses dance to tell a story

dress-up—to play dress-up means to put on fancy clothing and pretend to be someone else

doorbell—a bell or buzzer outside a door that is rung by someone who wants the door to be opened

ignore—to take no notice of something

pirate—a person who steals from ships at sea. pirates are sometimes characters in stories

shy—if someone is shy. he or she is bashful and does not feel comfortable around people or with strangers

stage—a raised platform on which actors and other entertainers perform

voice—the sound produced when you speak or sing

About the Author and Illustrator

Kim Kane is an award-winning author who writes for children and teens in Australia and overseas. Kim's books include the CBCA short-listed picture book *Family Forest* and her middle-grade novel *Pip: the Story of Olive*. Kim lives with her family in Melbourne and writes whenever and wherever she can.

Kim Kane

Pirates, old elephants, witches in bloomers, bears on bikes, ugly cats, sweet kids – Jon Davies does it all! Based in Twickenham, United Kingdom, Jon Davis has illustrated more than 40 kids' books for publishers across the globe.

Jon Davis

Collect them all!